Giovanni Boccaccio

Ten Tales from the Decameron

TRANSLATED BY G. H. McWILLIAM

PENGUIN BOOKS

PENGUIN BOOKS

Published by the Penguin Group
Penguin Books Ltd, 27 Wrights Lane, London w8 5tz, England
Penguin Books USA Inc., 375 Hudson Street, New York, New York 10014, USA
Penguin Books Australia Ltd, Ringwood, Victoria, Australia
Penguin Books Canada Ltd, 10 Alcorn Avenue, Toronto, Ontario, Canada m4v 3b2
Penguin Books (NZ) Ltd, 182–190 Wairau Road, Auckland 10, New Zealand

Penguin Books Ltd, Registered Offices: Harmondsworth, Middlesex, England

These stories are from the *Decameron* by Giovanni Boccaccio, translated by
G. H. McWilliam, revised edition published in Penguin Classics 1995
This edition published 1995
1 3 5 7 9 10 8 6 4 2

Typeset by Rowland Phototypesetting Ltd, Bury St Edmunds, Suffolk
Printed in England by Clays Ltd, St Ives plc

CONTENTS

In the summer of 1348, as a terrible plague
ravages the city, ten young Florentines seek refuge in the
surrounding countryside. To entertain themselves, they take
turns in telling each other stories. On each day, one
member of the group chooses a subject, and then all are
required to tell a tale embracing the chosen theme. Over ten
days, one hundred stories are told, and what follows
is a selection of those stories . . .

First Day

Not many years ago, there lived in Bologna a brilliant physician of almost universal renown, and perhaps he is alive to this day, whose name was Master Alberto. Although he was an old man approaching seventy, and the natural warmth had almost entirely departed from his body, his heart was so noble that he was not averse to welcoming the flames of love. One day, whilst attending a feast, he had seen a strikingly beautiful woman, a widow whose name, according to some accounts, was Malgherida de' Ghisolieri. He was mightily attracted by the lady, and, no differently than if he had been in the prime of his youth, he felt those flames so keenly in his mature old breast, that he never seemed able to sleep at night, unless in the course of the day he had seen the fair lady's fine and delectable features. Hence he began to pass regularly up and down in front of the lady's house, sometimes on foot and sometimes on horseback, depending on his mood. And accordingly both she and several other ladies

1

quickly divined his motive, and often jested with one another to see a man of such great age and wisdom caught in the toils of love. For the good ladies seemed to suppose that the delightful sensations of love could take root and thrive in no other place than the frivolous hearts of the young.

Master Alberto continued to pass up and down, and one Sunday, whilst the lady happened to be seated outside her front door with a number of other ladies, they caught sight of him in the distance, coming in their direction. Whereupon they all resolved, with the lady's agreement, to receive him and do him honour, and then make fun of him over this great passion of his. And that was precisely what they did. For they all stood up and invited him to accompany them into a cool walled garden, where they plied him with excellent wines and sweetmeats, and eventually they asked him, charmingly and with good grace, how it came about that he had fallen in love with this fair lady, when he was well aware that she was being courted by many a handsome, well-bred and sprightly young admirer. On hearing himself chided so politely, the doctor replied, smiling broadly:

'My lady, the fact that I am enamoured should not

excite the wonder of anyone who is wise, and especially not your own, because you are worthy of my love. For albeit old men are naturally deficient in the powers required for lovemaking, they do not necessarily lack a ready will, or a just appreciation of what should be loved. On the contrary, in this respect their longer experience gives them an advantage over the young. The hope which sustains an old man like myself in loving one who is loved, as you are, by many young men, is founded on what I have often observed in places where I have seen ladies eating lupins and leeks whilst taking a meal out of doors. For although no part of the leek is good, yet the part which is less objectionable and more pleasing to the palate is the root, which you ladies are generally drawn by some aberration of the appetite to hold in the hand while you eat the leaves, which are not only worthless, but have an unpleasant taste. How am I to know, my lady, whether you are not equally eccentric in choosing your lovers? For if this were so, I should be the one you would choose, and the others would be cast aside.'

The gentlewoman, who along with the others was feeling somewhat abashed, replied:

'Master Alberto, you have given us a charming and

very sound reproof for our presumptuousness. Your love is none the less precious to me, since it proceeds from so patently wise and excellent a man. And therefore, saving my honour, you are free to ask of me what you will, and regard it as yours.'

The doctor stood up with his companions, thanked the lady, took his leave of her amid much laughter and merriment, and departed.

Thus the lady, thinking she would score a victory, underestimated the object of her raillery and was herself defeated. And if you ladies are wise, you will guard against following her example.

Second Day

During the reign of the Marquis Azzo of Ferrara, a merchant whose name was Rinaldo d'Asti was returning home after dispatching certain business in Bologna. He had already passed through Ferrara, and was riding towards Verona, when he fell in with three men who, though they had the appearance of merchants, were in fact brigands of a particularly desperate and disreputable sort. With these he struck up conversation, and rashly agreed to ride along in their company.

On seeing that he was a merchant, who was probably carrying a certain amount of money with him, these men resolved to rob him at the earliest opportunity. But in order not to arouse his suspicions, they assumed an air of simplicity and respectability, restricting their conversation to the subject of loyalty and other polite topics, and went out of their way to appear humble and obliging towards him. He consequently thought himself very fortunate to have met

5

them, for he was travelling alone except for a single servant on horseback. As they went along, with the conversation passing as usual from one thing to another, they got on to the subject of the prayers that people address to God, and one of the bandits turned to Rinaldo and said:

'What about you, sir? What prayer do you generally say when you are travelling?'

'To tell the truth,' Rinaldo replied, 'in matters of this kind I am rather simple and down-to-earth. I am one of the old-fashioned sort who likes to call a spade a spade, and I don't know many prayers. All the same, when I am travelling it is my custom never to leave the inn of a morning without reciting an Our Father and a Hail Mary for the souls of Saint Julian's father and mother, after which I pray to God and the Saint to give me a good lodging for the night to come. On many a day, in the course of my travels, I have met with great dangers, only to survive them all and find myself at nightfall in a safe place and a comfortable lodging. Now I firmly believe this favour to have been obtained for me from God by Saint Julian, in whose honour I recite my prayer; and if on any morning I neglected to say it, I would feel I could do nothing right the whole day, and would come to some harm before the evening.'

'Did you say it this morning?' said the man who had asked him the question.

'I did indeed,' replied Rinaldo.

The man, who by this time knew what was going to happen, said to himself: 'A fat lot of good it will do you, for I reckon you are going to have a poor night's lodging if all goes according to plan.' Then he turned to Rinaldo and said:

'I too have travelled a great deal, and although I have heard many people speak highly of this Saint, I have never prayed to him myself. Nevertheless, I have always managed to find good quarters. Perhaps we shall see this evening which of us is the better lodged: you, who have said the prayer, or I, who have not said it. Mind you, I *do* use another one instead, either the *Dirupisti* or the *Intemerata* or the *De Profundis*, all of which are extremely effective, or so my old grandmother used to tell me.'

And so they went along, talking of this and that, with the three men biding their time and waiting for a suitable place to carry their villainous plan into effect. The day was drawing to a close when, at a concealed and deserted river-crossing on the far side of the fortress-town called Castel Guiglielmo, the three bandits took advantage of the lateness of the hour to launch their attack and rob him of everything he possessed, including his horse. Before leaving, they turned to him as he stood there in nothing but his shirt, and called out:

'Now see whether the prayer you said to Saint Julian will give you as good a night's lodging as our own saint will provide for us.' They then crossed the river, and rode off.

Rinaldo's wretch of a servant did nothing to assist his master on seeing him attacked, but turned his horse round and galloped all the way to Castel Guiglielmo without stopping. It was already dark by the time he entered the town, so he conveniently forgot the whole business, and put up for the night at an inn.

Rinaldo, bare-footed and wearing only a shirt, was at his wits' end, for the weather was very cold, it was snowing hard the whole time, and it was getting darker every minute. Shivering all over, his teeth chattering, he began to look round for a sheltered spot where he could spend the night without freezing to death. But since there had been a war in the countryside a short time previously and everything had been burnt to the ground, there was no shelter to be seen anywhere, and so he set off for Castel Guiglielmo, walking at a brisk pace on account of the cold. He had no idea whether his servant had fled to the fortress or to some other town, but he thought that, once inside the walls, God would surely send him some sort of relief.

He still had over a mile to go when night came on with a vengeance, and when he finally arrived it was so late that the gates were locked, the drawbridges were up, and he was unable to gain admittance. Feeling depressed and miserable, he looked round with tears in his eyes to see whether there was a place where he would at least find some protection from the snow, and he happened to catch sight of a house that jutted out appreciably from the top of the castle walls, so he decided to go and take refuge beneath it till daybreak. When he reached the spot, he discovered there was a postern underneath the overhang, and although the door was locked, at its base he heaped a quantity of straw which was lying nearby, and settled down upon it. He was thoroughly fed up, and complained at regular intervals to Saint Julian, saying that this was no way to treat one of his faithful devotees. Saint Julian had not lost sight of him, however, and before very long he was to see that Rinaldo was comfortably settled.

In the castle there was a widow, lovelier of body than any other woman in the world, with whom the Marquis Azzo was madly in love. He had set her up there as his mistress, and she was living in the very house beneath which Rinaldo had taken refuge. As it happened, the Marquis had arrived at the castle on that very day with the intention of spending the night with her, and had made secret arrangements to have a sumptuous supper prepared, and to take a bath in the lady's house beforehand. Everything was ready, and she was only waiting for the Marquis to turn up, when a servant happened to arrive at the gate, bringing the Marquis a message requiring him to leave immediately. So he sent word to the lady that he would not be coming, then hastily mounted his horse and rode away. The lady, feeling rather disconsolate and not knowing what to do with herself, decided she would have the bath which had been prepared for the Marquis, after which she would sup and go to bed. And so into the bath she went.

As she lay there in the bath, which was near the postern on the other side of which our unfortunate hero had taken shelter, she could hear the wails and moans being uttered by Rinaldo, who sounded from the way his teeth were chattering as if he had been turned into a stork. She therefore summoned her maid, and said:

'Go upstairs, look over the wall, and see who it is on the other side of this door. Find out who he is and what he is doing there.'

The maid went up, and by the light of the stars she saw him sitting there just as we have described him, bare-footed and wearing only his shirt, and quivering all over like a jelly. She asked him who he was, and Rinaldo, who was shaking so much that he could hardly articulate, told her his name and explained as briefly as possible how and why he came to be there. He then implored her, in an agonized voice, to do whatever she could to prevent his being left there all night slowly freezing to death.

The maid, feeling very sorry for him, returned to her mistress and told her the whole story. The lady too was filled with pity, and, remembering that she had a key for that particular door, which the Marquis occasionally used for his clandestine visits, she said to the maid:

'Go and let him in, but do it quietly. We have this supper here, and no one to eat it. And we can easily put him up, for there's plenty of room.'

The maid warmly commended her mistress's charity, then she went and opened the door and let him in. Perceiving that he was almost frozen stiff, the lady of the house said to him:

'Quickly, good sir, step into that bath whilst it is still warm.'

He willingly obeyed, without waiting to be bidden twice. His whole body was refreshed by its warmth, and he felt as if he were returning from death to life. The lady had him supplied with clothes that had once belonged to her husband, who had died quite recently, and when he put them on they fitted him to perfection. As he awaited further instructions from the lady, he fell to thanking God and Saint Julian for rescuing him from the cruel night he had been expecting, and leading him to what appeared a good lodging.

Meanwhile the lady had taken a brief rest, having first ordered a huge fire to be lit in one of the rooms, to which she presently came, asking what had become of the gentleman.

'He's dressed, ma'am,' replied the maid, 'and he's ever so handsome, and seems a very decent and respectable person.'

'Then go and call him,' said the woman, 'and tell him to come here by the fire and have some supper, for I know he has not had anything to eat.'

On entering the room, Rinaldo, judging from her appearance that she was a lady of quality, greeted her with due reverence and thanked her with all the eloquence at his command for the kindness she had done him. When she saw him and heard him speak, the lady concluded that her maid had been right, and she welcomed him cordially, installed him in a comfortable chair beside her own in front of the fire, and asked him what had happened and how he came to be there, whereupon Rinaldo told her the whole story in detail.

The lady had already heard bits of the story after the arrival of Rinaldo's servant at the castle, and so she fully believed everything he told him. She in turn told him what she knew about his servant, adding that it would be easy enough to find him next morning. But by now the table was laid for supper, and Rinaldo, after washing his hands with the lady, accepted her invitation to sit down and eat at her side.

He was a fine, tall, handsome fellow in the prime of manhood, with impeccably good manners, and the lady cast many an appreciative glance in his direction. As she had been expecting to sleep with the Marquis, her carnal instincts were already aroused, and after supper she got up from the table and consulted with her maid to find out whether she thought it a good idea, since the Marquis had let her down, to make use of this unexpected gift of Fortune. The maid, knowing what her mistress had in mind, encouraged her for all she was worth, with the result that the lady returned to Rinaldo, whom she had left standing alone by the fire, and began to ogle him, saying:

'Come, Rinaldo, why are you looking so unhappy? What's the good of worrying about the loss of a horse and a few clothes? Do relax and cheer up. I want you to feel completely at home here. In fact, I will go so far as to say that seeing you in those clothes, I keep thinking you are my late husband, and I've been wanting to take you in my arms and kiss you the whole evening. I would certainly have done so, but I was afraid you might take it amiss.'

On hearing these words and perceiving the gleam in the lady's eyes, Rinaldo, who was no fool, advanced towards her with open arms, saying:

'My lady, I shall always have you to thank for the fact that I am alive, and when I consider the fate from which you delivered me, it would be highly discourteous of me if I did not attempt to further your inclinations to the best of my ability. Kiss and embrace me, therefore, to your heart's content, and I shall be more than happy to return the compliment.'

There was no need for any further preliminaries. The lady, who was all aflame with amorous desire, promptly rushed into his arms. Clasping him to her bosom, she smothered him with a thousand eager kisses and received as many in return, then they both retired into her bedroom, where they lost no time in getting into bed, and before the night was over they satisfied their longings repeatedly and in full measure.

They arose as soon as dawn began to break, for the lady was anxious not to give cause for scandal. Having provided him with some very old clothes and filled his purse with money, she then explained which road he must take on entering the fortress in order to find his servant, and finally she let him out by the postern through which he had entered, imploring him to keep their encounter a secret.

As soon as it was broad day and the gates were opened, he entered the castle, giving the impression he was arriving from a distance, and rooted out his servant. Having changed into the clothes that were in his portmanteau, he was about to mount his servant's horse, when as if by some divine miracle the three brigands were brought into the castle, after being arrested for another crime they had committed shortly after robbing him on the previous evening. They had made a voluntary confession, and consequently Rinaldo's horse, clothing and money were restored to him, and all he lost was a pair of garters, which the robbers were unable to account for.

Thus it was that Rinaldo, giving thanks to God and Saint Julian, mounted his horse and returned home safe and sound, whilst the three robbers went next day to dangle their heels in the north wind.

Third Day

TENTH STORY

There once lived in the town of Gafsa, in Barbary, a very rich man who had numerous children, among them a lovely and graceful young daughter called Alibech. She was not herself a Christian, but there were many Christians in the town, and one day, having on occasion heard them extol the Christian faith and the service of God, she asked one of them for his opinion on the best and easiest way for a person to 'serve God', as they put it. He answered her by saying that the ones who served God best were those who put the greatest distance between themselves and earthly goods, as happened in the case of people who had gone to live in the remoter parts of the Sahara.

She said no more about it to anyone, but next morning, being a very simple-natured creature of fourteen or thereabouts, Alibech set out all alone, in secret, and made her way towards the desert, prompted by nothing more logical than a strong adolescent impulse. A few days later, exhausted from fatigue and hunger, she arrived in the heart of the wilderness, where, catching sight of a small hut in the distance, she stumbled towards it, and in the doorway she found a holy man, who was astonished to see her in those parts and asked her what she was doing there. She told him that she had been inspired by God, and that she was trying, not only to serve Him, but also to find someone who could teach her how she should go about it.

On observing how young and exceedingly pretty she was, the good man was afraid to take her under his wing lest the devil should catch him unawares. So he praised her for her good intentions, and having given her a quantity of herb-roots, wild apples and dates to eat, and some water to drink, he said to her:

'My daughter, not very far from here there is a holy man who is much more capable than I of teaching you what you want to know. Go along to him.' And he sent her upon her way.

When she came to this second man, she was told precisely the same thing, and so she went on until she arrived at the cell of a young hermit, a very devout and kindly fellow called Rustico, to whom she put the same inquiry as she had addressed to the others. Being anxious to prove to himself that he possessed a will of iron, he did not, like the others, send her away or direct her elsewhere, but kept her with him in his cell, in a corner of which, when night descended, he prepared a makeshift bed out of palm-leaves, upon which he invited her to lie down and rest.

Once he had taken this step, very little time elapsed before temptation went to war against his willpower, and after the first few assaults, finding himself outmanoeuvred on all fronts, he laid down his arms and surrendered. Casting aside pious thoughts, prayers, and penitential exercises, he began to concentrate his mental faculties upon the youth and beauty of the girl, and to devise suitable ways and means for approaching her in such a fashion that she should not think it lewd of him to make the sort of proposal he had in mind. By putting certain questions to her, he soon discovered that she had never been intimate with the opposite sex and was every bit as innocent as she seemed; and he therefore thought of a possible way to persuade her, with the pretext of serving God, to grant his desires. He began by delivering a long speech in which he showed her how powerful an enemy the devil was to the Lord God, and followed this up by impressing upon her that of all the ways of serving God, the one that He most appreciated consisted in putting the devil back in Hell, to which the Almighty had consigned him in the first place.

The girl asked him how this was done, and Rustico replied:

'You will soon find out, but just do whatever you see me doing for the present.' And so saying, he began to divest himself of the few clothes he was wearing, leaving himself completely naked. The girl followed his example, and he sank to his knees as though he were about to pray, getting her to kneel directly opposite.

In this posture, the girl's beauty was displayed to Rustico in all its glory, and his longings blazed more fiercely than ever, bringing about the resurrection of the flesh. Alibech stared at this in amazement, and said:

'Rustico, what is that thing I see sticking out in front of you, which I do not possess?'

'Oh, my daughter,' said Rustico, 'this is the devil I was telling you about. Do you see what he's doing? He's hurting me so much that I can hardly endure it.'

'Oh, praise be to God,' said the girl, 'I can see that I am better off than you are, for I have no such devil to contend with.'

'You're right there,' said Rustico. 'But you have something else instead, that I haven't.'

'Oh?' said Alibech. 'And what's that?'

'You have Hell,' said Rustico. 'And I honestly believe that God has sent you here for the salvation of my soul, because if this devil continues to plague the life out of me, and if you are prepared to take sufficient pity upon me to let me put him back into Hell, you will be giving me marvellous relief, as well as rendering incalculable service and pleasure to God, which is what you say you came here for in the first place.'

'Oh, Father,' replied the girl in all innocence, 'if I really do have a Hell, let's do as you suggest just as soon as you are ready.'

'God bless you, my daughter,' said Rustico. 'Let us go and put him back, and then perhaps he'll leave me alone.'

At which point he conveyed the girl to one of their beds, where he instructed her in the art of incarcerating that accursed fiend.

Never having put a single devil into Hell before, the girl found the first experience a little painful, and she said to Rustico:

'This devil must certainly be a bad lot, Father, and a true enemy of God, for as well as plaguing mankind, he even hurts Hell when he's driven back inside it.'

'Daughter,' said Rustico, 'it will not always be like that.' And in order to ensure that it wouldn't, before moving from the bed they put him back half a dozen times, curbing his arrogance to such good effect that he was positively glad to keep still for the rest of the day.

During the next few days, however, the devil's pride frequently reared its head again, and the girl, ever ready to obey the call to duty and bring him under control, happened to develop a taste for the sport, and began saying to Rustico:

'I can certainly see what those worthy men in Gafsa meant when they said that serving God was so agreeable. I don't honestly recall ever having done anything that gave me so much pleasure and satisfaction as I get from putting the devil back in Hell. To my way of thinking, anyone who devotes his energies to anything but the service of God is a complete blockhead.'

She thus developed the habit of going to Rustico at frequent intervals, and saying to him:

'Father, I came here to serve God, not to idle away my time. Let's go and put the devil back in Hell.'

And sometimes, in the middle of their labours, she would say:

'What puzzles me, Rustico, is that the devil should ever want to escape from Hell. Because if he liked being there as much as Hell enjoys receiving him and keeping him inside, he would never go away at all.'

By inviting Rustico to play the game too often, continually urging him on in the service of God, the girl took so much stuffing out of him that he eventually began to turn cold where another man would have been bathed in sweat. So he told her that the devil should only be punished and put back in Hell when he reared his head with pride, adding that by the grace of Heaven, they had tamed him so effectively that he was pleading with God to be left in peace. In this way, he managed to keep the girl quiet for a while, but one day, having begun to notice that Rustico was no longer asking for the devil to be put back in Hell, she said:

'Look here, Rustico. Even though your devil has been punished and pesters you no longer, my Hell simply refuses to leave me alone. Now that I have helped you with my Hell to subdue the pride of your devil, the least you can do is to get your devil to help me tame the fury of my Hell.'

Rustico, who was living on a diet of herb-roots and water, was quite incapable of supplying her requirements, and told her that the taming of her Hell would require an awful lot of devils, but promised to do what he could. Sometimes, therefore, he responded to the call, but this happened so infrequently that it was rather like chucking a bean into the mouth of a lion, with the result that the girl, who felt that she was not serving God as diligently as she would have liked, was found complaining more often than not.

But at the height of this dispute between Alibech's Hell and Rustico's devil, brought about by a surplus of desire on the one hand and a shortage of power on the other, a fire broke out in Gafsa, and Alibech's father was burnt to death in his own house along with all his children and every other member of his household, so that Alibech inherited the whole of his property. Because of this a young man called Neerbal who had spent the whole of his substance in sumptuous living, having heard that she was still alive, set out to look for her, and before the authorities were able to appropriate her late father's fortune on the grounds that there was no heir, he succeeded in tracing her whereabouts. To the great relief of Rustico, but against her own wishes, he took her back to Gafsa and married her, thus inheriting a half-share in her father's enormous fortune.

Before Neerbal had actually slept with her, she was questioned by the women of Gafsa about how she had served God in the desert, and she replied that she had served Him by putting the devil back in Hell, and that Neerbal had committed a terrible sin by stopping her from performing so worthy a service.

'How do you put the devil back in Hell?' asked the women.

Partly in words and partly through gestures, the girl showed them how it was done, whereupon the women laughed so much that they are laughing yet; and they said:

'Don't let it worry you, my dear. People do the job every bit as well here in Gafsa, and Neerbal will give you plenty of help in serving the Lord.'

The story was repeated throughout the town, being passed from one woman to the next, and they coined a proverbial saying there to the effect that the most agreeable way of serving God was to put the devil back in Hell. The dictum later crossed the sea to Italy, where it survives to this day.

And so, young ladies, if you stand in need of God's grace, see that you learn to put the devil back in Hell, for it is greatly to His liking and pleasurable to the parties concerned, and a great deal of good can arise and flow in the process.

Fourth Day

In Messina, there once lived three brothers, all of them merchants who had been left very rich after the death of their father, whose native town was San Gimignano. They had a sister called Lisabetta, but for some reason or other they had failed to bestow her in marriage, despite the fact that she was uncommonly gracious and beautiful.

In one of their trading establishments, the three brothers employed a young Pisan named Lorenzo, who planned and directed all their operations, and who, being rather dashing and handsomely proportioned, had often attracted the gaze of Lisabetta. Having noticed more than once that she had grown exceedingly fond of him, Lorenzo abandoned all his other amours and began in like fashion to set his own heart on winning Lisabetta. And since they were equally in love with each other, before very long they gratified their dearest wishes, taking care not to be discovered.

In this way, their love continued to prosper, much

to their common enjoyment and pleasure. They did everything they could to keep the affair a secret, but one night, as Lisabetta was making her way to Lorenzo's sleeping-quarters, she was observed, without knowing it, by her eldest brother. The discovery greatly distressed him, but being a young man of some intelligence, and not wishing to do anything that would bring discredit upon his family, he neither spoke nor made a move, but spent the whole of the night applying his mind to various sides of the matter.

Next morning he described to his brothers what he had seen of Lisabetta and Lorenzo the night before, and the three of them talked the thing over at considerable length. Being determined that the affair should leave no stain upon the reputation either of themselves or of their sister, he decided that they must pass it over in silence and pretend to have neither seen nor heard anything until such time as it was safe and convenient for them to rid themselves of this ignominy before it got out of hand.

Abiding by this decision, the three brothers jested and chatted with Lorenzo in their usual manner, until one day they pretended they were all going off on a pleasure-trip to the country, and took Lorenzo with them. They bided their time, and on reaching a very remote and lonely spot, they took Lorenzo off his guard, murdered him, and buried his corpse. No one had witnessed the deed, and on their return to Messina they put it about that they had sent Lorenzo away on a trading assignment, being all the more readily believed as they had done this so often before.

Lorenzo's continued absence weighed heavily upon Lisabetta, who kept asking her brothers, in anxious tones, what had become of him, and eventually her questioning became so persistent that one of her brothers rounded on her, and said:

'What is the meaning of this? What business do you have with Lorenzo, that you should be asking so many questions about him? If you go on pestering us, we shall give you the answer you deserve.'

From then on, the young woman, who was sad and miserable and full of strange forebodings, refrained from asking questions. But at night she would repeatedly utter his name in a heart-rending voice and beseech him to come to her, and from time to time she would burst into tears because of his failure to return. Nothing would restore her spirits, and meanwhile she simply went on waiting.

One night, however, after crying so much over Lorenzo's absence that she eventually cried herself off to sleep, he appeared to her in a dream, pallid-looking and all dishevelled, his clothes tattered and decaying, and it seemed to her that he said:

'Ah, Lisabetta, you do nothing but call to me and bemoan my long absence, and you cruelly reprove me with your tears. Hence I must tell you that I can never return, because on the day that you saw me for the last time, I was murdered by your brothers.'

He then described the place where they had buried him, told her not to call to him or wait for him any longer, and disappeared.

Having woken up, believing that what she had seen was true, the young woman wept bitterly. And when she arose next morning, she resolved to go to the place and seek confirmation of what she had seen in her sleep. She dared not mention the apparition to her brothers, but obtained their permission to make a brief trip to the country for pleasure, taking with her a maid-servant who had once acted as her go-between and was privy to all her affairs. She immediately set out, and on reaching the spot, swept aside some dead leaves and started to excavate a section of the ground that appeared to have been disturbed. Nor did she have to dig very deep before she uncovered her poor lover's body, which, showing no sign as yet of decomposition or decay, proved all too clearly that her vision had been true. She was the saddest woman alive, but knowing that this was no time for weeping, and seeing that it was impossible for her to take away his whole body (as she would dearly have wished), she laid it to rest in a more appropriate spot, then severed the head from the shoulders as best she could and enveloped it in a towel. This she handed into her maidservant's keeping whilst she covered over the remainder of the corpse with soil, and then they returned home, having completed the whole of their task unobserved.

Taking the head to her room, she locked herself in and cried bitterly, weeping so profusely that she saturated it with her tears, at the same time implanting a thousand kisses upon it. Then she wrapped the head in a piece of rich cloth, and laid it in a large and elegant pot, of the sort in which basil or marjoram is grown. She next covered it with soil, in which she planted several sprigs of the finest Salernitan basil, and never watered them except with essence of roses or orange-blossom, or with her own teardrops. She took to sitting permanently beside this pot and gazing lovingly at it, concentrating the whole of her desire upon it because it was where her beloved Lorenzo lay concealed. And after gazing raptly for a long while upon it, she would bend over it and begin to cry, and her weeping never ceased until the whole of the basil was wet with her tears.

Because of the long and unceasing care that was lavished upon it, and also because the soil was enriched by the decomposing head inside the pot, the basil grew very thick and exceedingly fragrant. The young woman constantly followed this same routine, and from time to time she attracted the attention of her neighbours. And as they had heard her brothers expressing their concern at the decline in her good looks and the way in which her eyes appeared to have sunk into their sockets, they told them what they had seen, adding:

'We have noticed that she follows the same routine every day.'

The brothers discovered for themselves that this was so, and having reproached her once or twice without the slightest effect, they caused the pot to be secretly removed from her room. When she found that it was missing, she kept asking for it over and over again, and because they would not restore it to her she sobbed and cried without a pause until eventually she fell seriously ill. And from her bed of sickness she would call for nothing else except her pot of basil.

The young men were astonished by the persistence of her entreaties, and decided to examine its contents. Having shaken out the soil, they saw the cloth and found the decomposing head inside it, still sufficiently intact for them to recognize it as Lorenzo's from the curls of his hair. This discovery greatly amazed them, and they were afraid lest people should come to know what had happened. So they buried the head, and without breathing a word to anyone, having wound up their affairs in Messina, they left the city and went to live in Naples.

The girl went on weeping and demanding her pot of basil, until eventually she cried herself to death, thus bringing her ill-fated love to an end. But after due process of time, many people came to know of the affair, and one of them composed the song which can still be heard to this day:

> Whoever it was,
> Whoever the villain
> That stole my pot of herbs, etc.

Fifth Day

You are to know, then, that Coppo di Borghese Domenichi, who once used to live in our city and possibly lives there still, one of the most highly respected men of our century, a person worthy of eternal fame, who achieved his position of pre-eminence by dint of his character and abilities rather than by his noble lineage, frequently took pleasure during his declining years in discussing incidents from the past with his neighbours and other folk. In this pastime he excelled all others, for he was more coherent, possessed a superior memory, and spoke with greater eloquence. He had a fine repertoire, including a tale he frequently told concerning a young Florentine called Federigo, the son of Messer Filippo Alberighi, who for his deeds of chivalry and courtly manners was more highly spoken of than any other squire in Tuscany. In the manner of most young men of gentle breeding, Federigo lost his heart to a noble lady, whose name was Monna Giovanna, and who in her time was considered one

34

of the loveliest and most adorable women to be found in Florence. And with the object of winning her love, he rode at the ring, tilted, gave sumptuous banquets, and distributed a large number of gifts, spending money without any restraint whatsoever. But since she was no less chaste than she was fair, the lady took no notice, either of the things that were done in her honour, or of the person who did them.

In this way, spending far more than he could afford and deriving no profit in return, Federigo lost his entire fortune (as can easily happen) and reduced himself to poverty, being left with nothing other than a tiny little farm, which produced an income just sufficient for him to live very frugally, and one falcon of the finest breed in the whole world. Since he was as deeply in love as ever, and felt unable to go on living the sort of life in Florence to which he aspired, he moved out to Campi, where his little farm happened to be situated. Having settled in the country, he went hunting as often as possible with his falcon, and, without seeking assistance from anyone, he patiently resigned himself to a life of poverty.

Now one day, while Federigo was living in these straitened circumstances, the husband of Monna

Giovanna happened to fall ill, and, realizing that he was about to die, he drew up his will. He was a very rich man, and in his will he left everything to his son, who was just growing up, further stipulating that, if his son should die without legitimate issue, his estate should go to Monna Giovanna, to whom he had always been deeply devoted.

Shortly afterwards he died, leaving Monna Giovanna a widow, and every summer, in accordance with Florentine custom, she went away with her son to a country estate of theirs, which was very near Federigo's farm. Consequently this young lad of hers happened to become friendly with Federigo, acquiring a passion for birds and dogs; and, having often seen Federigo's falcon in flight, he became fascinated by it and longed to own it, but since he could see that Federigo was deeply attached to the bird, he never ventured to ask him for it.

And there the matter rested, when, to the consternation of his mother, the boy happened to be taken ill. Being her only child, he was the apple of his mother's eye, and she sat beside his bed the whole day long, never ceasing to comfort him. Every so often she asked him whether there was anything he wanted, imploring him to tell her what it was, because if it was possible to acquire it, she would move heaven and earth to obtain it for him.

After hearing this offer repeated for the umpteenth time, the boy said:

'Mother, if you could arrange for me to have Federigo's falcon, I believe I should soon get better.'

On hearing this request, the lady was somewhat taken aback, and began to consider what she could do about it. Knowing that Federigo had been in love with her for a long time, and that she had never deigned to cast so much as a single glance in his direction, she said to herself: 'How can I possibly go to him, or even send anyone, to ask him for this falcon, which to judge from all I have heard is the finest that ever flew, as well as being the only thing that keeps him alive? And how can I be so heartless as to deprive so noble a man of his one remaining pleasure?'

Her mind filled with reflections of this sort, she remained silent, not knowing what answer to make to her son's request, even though she was quite certain that the falcon was hers for the asking.

At length, however, her maternal instincts gained the upper hand, and she resolved, come what may, to satisfy the child by going in person to Federigo to collect the bird and bring it back to him. And so she replied:

'Bear up, my son, and see whether you can start feeling any better. I give you my word that I shall go and fetch it for you first thing tomorrow morning.'

Next morning, taking another lady with her for company, his mother left the house as though intending to go for a walk, made her way to Federigo's little cottage, and asked to see him. For several days, the weather had been unsuitable for hawking, so Federigo was attending to one or two little jobs in his garden, and when he heard, to his utter astonishment, that Monna Giovanna was at the front door and wished to speak to him, he happily rushed there to greet her.

When she saw him coming, she advanced with womanly grace to meet him. Federigo received her with a deep bow, whereupon she said:

'Greetings, Federigo!' Then she continued: 'I have come to make amends for the harm you have suffered on my account, by loving me more than you ought to have done. As a token of my esteem, I should like to take breakfast with you this morning, together with my companion here, but you must not put yourself to any trouble.'

'My lady,' replied Federigo in all humility, 'I cannot recall ever having suffered any harm on your account. On the contrary I have gained so much that if ever I attained any kind of excellence, it was entirely because of your own great worth and the love I bore you. Moreover I can assure you that this visit which you have been generous enough to pay me is worth more to me than all the money I ever possessed, though I fear that my hospitality will not amount to very much.'

So saying, he led her unassumingly into the house, and thence into his garden, where, since there was no one else he could call upon to chaperon her, he said:

'My lady, as there is nobody else available, this good woman, who is the wife of the farmer here, will keep you company whilst I go and see about setting the table.'

Though his poverty was acute, the extent to which he had squandered his wealth had not yet been fully borne home to Federigo; but on this particular morning, finding that he had nothing to set before the lady for whose love he had entertained so lavishly in the past, his eyes were well and truly opened to the fact.

Distressed beyond all measure, he silently cursed his bad luck and rushed all over the house like one possessed, but could find no trace of either money or valuables. By now the morning was well advanced, he was still determined to entertain the gentlewoman to some sort of meal, and, not wishing to beg assistance from his own farmer (or from anyone else, for that matter), his gaze alighted on his precious falcon, which was sitting on its perch in the little room where it was kept. And having discovered, on picking it up, that it was nice and plump, he decided that since he had nowhere else to turn, it would make a worthy dish for such a lady as this. So without thinking twice about it he wrung the bird's neck and promptly handed it over to his housekeeper to be plucked, dressed, and roasted carefully on a spit. Then he covered the table with spotless linen, of which he still had a certain amount in his possession, and returned in high spirits to the garden, where he announced to his lady that the meal, such as he had been able to prepare, was now ready.

The lady and her companion rose from where they were sitting and made their way to the table. And together with Federigo, who waited on them with the utmost deference, they made a meal of the prize falcon without knowing what they were eating.

On leaving the table they engaged their host in pleasant conversation for a while, and when the lady thought it time to broach the subject she had gone there to discuss, she turned to Federigo and addressed him affably as follows:

'I do not doubt for a moment, Federigo, that you will be astonished at my impertinence when you discover my principal reason for coming here, especially when you recall your former mode of living and my virtue, which you possibly mistook for harshness and cruelty. But if you had ever had any children to make you appreciate the power of parental love, I should think it certain that you would to some extent forgive me.

'However, the fact that you have no children of your own does not exempt me, a mother, from the laws common to all other mothers. And being bound to obey those laws, I am forced, contrary to my own wishes and to all the rules of decorum and propriety, to ask you for something to which I know you are very deeply attached – which is only natural, seeing that it is the only consolation, the only pleasure, the only recreation remaining to you in your present extremity of fortune. The gift I am seeking is your falcon, to which my son has taken so powerful a liking, that if I fail to take it to him I fear he will succumb to the illness from which he is suffering, and consequently I shall lose him. In imploring you to give me this falcon, I appeal, not to your love, for you are under no obligation to me on that account, but rather to your noble heart, whereby you have proved yourself superior to all others in the practice of courtesy. Do me this favour, then, so that I may claim that through your generosity I have saved my son's life, thus placing him forever in your debt.'

When he heard what it was that she wanted, and realized that he could not oblige her because he had given her the falcon to eat, Federigo burst into tears in her presence before being able to utter a single word in reply. At first the lady thought his tears stemmed more from his grief at having to part with his fine falcon than from any other motive, and was on the point of telling him that she would prefer not to have it. But on second thoughts she said nothing, and waited for Federigo to stop crying and give her his answer, which eventually he did.

'My lady,' he said, 'ever since God decreed that you should become the object of my love, I have repeatedly had cause to complain of Fortune's hostility towards me. But all her previous blows were slight by comparison with the one she has dealt me now. Nor shall I ever be able to forgive her, when I reflect that you have come to my poor dwelling, which you never deigned to visit when it was rich, and that you desire from me a trifling favour which she has made it impossible for me to concede. The reason is simple, and I shall explain it in few words.

'When you did me the kindness of telling me that you wished to breakfast with me, I considered it right and proper, having regard to your excellence and merit, to do everything within my power to prepare a more sumptuous dish than those I would offer to any ordinary guest. My thoughts therefore turned to the falcon you have asked me for and, knowing its quality, I reputed it a worthy dish to set before you. So I had it roasted and served to you on the trencher this morning, and I could not have wished for a better way of disposing of it. But now that I discover that you wanted it in a different form, I am so distressed by my inability to grant your request that I shall never forgive myself for as long as I live.'

In confirmation of his words, Federigo caused the feathers, talons and beak to be cast on the table before her. On seeing and hearing all this, the lady reproached him at first for killing so fine a falcon, and serving it up for a woman to eat; but then she became lost in admiration for his magnanimity of spirit, which no amount of poverty had managed to diminish, nor ever would. But now that her hopes of obtaining the falcon had vanished she began to feel seriously concerned for the health of her son, and after thanking Federigo for his hospitality and good intentions, she took her leave of him, looking all despondent, and returned to the child. And to his mother's indescribable sorrow, within the space of a few days, whether through his disappointment in not being able to have the falcon, or because he was in any case suffering from a mortal illness, the child passed from this life.

After a period of bitter mourning and continued weeping, the lady was repeatedly urged by her brothers to remarry, since not only had she been left a vast fortune but she was still a young woman. And though she would have preferred to remain a widow, they gave her so little peace that in the end, recalling Federigo's high merits and his latest act of generosity, namely to have killed such a fine falcon in her honour, she said to her brothers:

'If only it were pleasing to you, I should willingly remain as I am; but since you are so eager for me to take a husband, you may be certain that I shall never marry any other man except Federigo degli Alberighi.'

Her brothers made fun of her, saying:

'Silly girl, don't talk such nonsense! How can you marry a man who hasn't a penny with which to bless himself?'

'My brothers,' she replied, 'I am well aware of that. But I would sooner have a gentleman without riches, than riches without a gentleman.'

Seeing that her mind was made up, and knowing Federigo to be a gentleman of great merit even though he was poor, her brothers fell in with her wishes and handed her over to him, along with her immense fortune. Thenceforth, finding himself married to this great lady with whom he was so deeply in love, and very rich into the bargain, Federigo managed his affairs more prudently, and lived with her in happiness to the end of his days.

Sixth Day

As all of you will have heard and seen for yourselves, Currado Gianfigliazzi has always played a notable part in the affairs of our city. Generous and hospitable, he lived the life of a true gentleman, and, to say nothing for the moment of his more important activities, he took a constant delight in hunting and hawking. One day, having killed a crane with one of his falcons in the vicinity of Peretola, finding that it was young and plump, he sent it to an excellent Venetian cook of his, whose name was Chichibio, telling him to roast it for supper and to see that it was well prepared and seasoned.

Chichibio, who was no less scatterbrained than he looked, plucked the crane, stuffed it, set it over the fire, and began to cook it with great care. But when it was nearly done, and giving off a most appetizing smell, there came into the kitchen a fair young country wench called Brunetta, who was the apple of Chichibio's eye. And on sniffing the smell of cooking and

46

seeing the crane roasting on the spit, she coaxed and pleaded with him to give her one of the legs. By way of reply, Chichibio burst into song:

'I won't let you have it, Donna Brunetta, I won't let you have it, so there!'

This put Donna Brunetta's back up, and she said:

'I swear to God that if you don't let me have it, you'll never have another thing out of me!' In short, they had quite a lengthy set-to, and in the end, not wishing to anger his girl, Chichibio cut off one of the crane's legs and gave it to her.

A little later, the crane was set before Currado and his guests, and much to his surprise, Currado found that one of the legs was missing. So he sent for Chichibio and asked him what had happened to it. Being a Venetian, and hence a good liar, Chichibio promptly replied:

'My lord, cranes have only the one leg.'

Whereupon Currado flew into a rage, and said:

'What the devil do you mean, cranes have only the one leg? Do you think I've never seen a crane before?'

'What I mean, sir,' continued Chichibio, 'is that they have only the one leg. We'll go and see some live ones, if you like, and I'll show you.'

Not wishing to embarrass his visitors, Currado decided not to pursue the matter, but said:

'I've never seen a one-legged crane before, nor have I ever heard of one. But since you have offered to show me, you can do so tomorrow morning, and then I shall be satisfied. But I swear to you by the body of Christ that if you fail to prove it, I shall see that you are given such a hiding that you will never forget my name for as long as you live.'

There the matter rested for that evening, but next morning, as soon as it was light, Currado, whom a night's sleep had done nothing to pacify, leapt out of bed, still seething with anger, and ordered his horses to be saddled. And, having obliged Chichibio to mount an old jade, he led the way to a river bank where cranes were usually to be seen in the early morning, saying:

'We shall soon see which of us was lying last night.'

On perceiving that Currado was still as angry as ever, and that he would now have to prove what he had said, Chichibio, who had no idea how he was going to do it, rode along behind Currado in a state of positive terror. If he could have run away he would gladly have done so, but since that was out of the question, he kept gazing ahead of him, behind him, and to each side, and wherever he looked he imagined he could see cranes standing on two legs.

However, just as they were approaching the river, Chichibio caught sight of well over a dozen cranes, all standing on one leg on the river bank, which is their normal posture when they are asleep. So he quickly pointed them out to Currado, saying:

'Now you can see quite plainly, sir, that I was telling you the truth last night when I said that cranes have only the one leg. Take a look at the ones over there.'

'Wait a bit,' said Currado, 'and I'll show you they have two.' And moving a little closer to them, he yelled: 'Oho!' whereupon the cranes lowered their other leg, and after taking a few strides, they all began to fly away. Currado then turned to Chichibio, saying:

'What do you say to that, you knave? Do they have two legs, or do they not?'

Chichibio was almost at his wits' end, but in some mysterious way he suddenly thought of an answer.

'They do indeed, sir,' he said, 'but you never shouted "Oho!" to the one you had last night, otherwise it would have shoved its second leg out, like these others.'

Currado was so delighted with this answer that

all his anger was converted into jollity and laughter.

'You're right, Chichibio,' he said. 'Of course, I should have shouted.'

This, then, was how Chichibio, with his prompt and amusing reply, avoided an unpleasant fate and made his peace with his master.

Seventh Day

SECOND STORY

Not so long ago, in Naples, a poor man took to wife a charming and beautiful girl, whose name was Peronella. He was a bricklayer by trade, and earned a very low wage, but this, together with the modest amount she earned from her spinning, was just about sufficient for them to live on.

Now one day, Peronella caught the eye of a sprightly young gallant, who, finding her exceedingly attractive, promptly fell in love with her, and by using all his powers of persuasion, he succeeded in gaining her acquaintance. So that they could be together, they came to this arrangement: that since her husband got up early every morning to go to work or to go and look for a job, the young man should lie in wait until he saw him leaving the house; and as the district where she lived, which was called Avorio, was very out-of-the-way, as soon as the husband had left, he should go in to her. And in this way they met very regularly.

But one particular morning, shortly after the good

man had left the house and Giannello Scrignario (such was the young gallant's name) had gone inside to join Peronella, the husband, who was usually away for the whole day, returned home. Finding the door locked on the inside, he knocked, and after he had knocked he said to himself:

'May the Lord God be forever praised; for though He has willed that I should be poor, at least He has given me the consolation of a good, chaste girl for a wife. See how quick she was to lock the door after I left, so that no one should come in and give her any trouble.'

Now, Peronella knew it was her husband from his way of knocking, and she said:

'O alas, Giannello my love, I'm done for! That's my husband, curse the fellow, who for some reason or other has come back home. I've never known him to return at this hour before; perhaps he saw you coming in. But whatever the reason, for God's sake hop into this tub over here while I go and let him in and find out what has brought him home so early in the day.'

Giannello promptly got into the tub, whereupon Peronella went and opened the door to her husband, and, pulling a long face, she said:

'What's got into you this morning, coming back home so early? It looks to me, seeing that you're carrying your tools, as if you've decided to take the day off, in which case what are we going to live on? How are we to buy anything to eat? Do you think I'm going to let you pawn my Sunday dress and my other little bits and pieces? Here I am, stuck in this house from morning till night and working my fingers to the bone, so that we shall at least have sufficient oil to keep our lamp alight! Oh, what a husband! I haven't a single neighbour who doesn't gape and laugh at me for slaving away as I do; and yet you come back here twiddling your thumbs when you ought to be out working.'

At this point she burst into tears, then started all over again, saying:

'O alas, woe is me, why was I ever born, what did I do to deserve such a husband? I could have had a decent, hard-working young fellow, and I turned him down to marry this worthless good-for-nothing, who doesn't appreciate what a good wife I am to him. All the other wives have a jolly good time: they have two or three lovers apiece, and they whoop it up under their husbands' noses, whereas for poor little me, just because I am a respectable woman and find that sort of thing distasteful, there's nothing but misery and ill luck. I just can't understand why I don't take one or two lovers, as other women do. It's time you realized, husband, that if I wanted to misbehave, I'd soon find someone to do it with, for there are plenty of sprightly young fellows who love and admire me, and who have offered me large sums of money, or dresses and jewels if I preferred, but not being the daughter of that kind of woman, I never had it in me to accept. And what is my reward? A husband who slopes back home when he ought to be out working.'

'Oh, for Heaven's sake, woman,' said her husband, 'stop making such a song and dance about it. I know how virtuous you are, and as a matter of fact I saw the proof of it this very morning. The fact is that I went to work, but what you don't seem to realize, and I didn't either, is that today is the feast of Saint Galeone and everybody's on holiday, and that's the reason I came home so early. But even so I've made sure that we shall have enough food to last us for over a month. You know that tub that's been cluttering up the house for ages? Well, I've sold it for five silver ducats to this man waiting here on the doorstep.'

Whereupon Peronella said:

'That really does put the lid on it. One would think that since you are a man and get about a good deal, you ought to know the value of things; yet you sell a tub for five silver ducats, which I, a mere woman who hardly ever puts her nose outside the front door, seeing what a nuisance it was to have it in the house, have just sold to an honest fellow here for seven ducats. He's inside the tub now, as a matter of fact, seeing whether it is sound.'

When he heard this, her husband was delighted, and turning to the man who had come to collect the tub, he said:

'Run along now, there's a good fellow. You heard what my wife said. She's sold it for seven, and all you would offer me for it was five.'

'So be it,' said the good fellow, and away he went.

And Peronella said to her husband:

'Now that you are here, you'd better come up and settle this with him yourself.'

Giannello was listening with both ears to see whether there was anything he had to guard against or attend to, and on hearing Peronella's words, he leapt smartly out of the tub. And with a casual sort of air, as though he had heard nothing of the husband's return, he called out:

'Are you there, good woman?'

Whereupon the husband, who was just coming up, said:

'Here I am, what can I do for you?'

'Who the hell are you?' said Giannello. 'It's the woman who was selling me this tub that I wanted to speak to.'

'That's all right,' said the good man. 'You can deal with me: I'm her husband.'

So Giannello said:

'The tub seems to be in pretty good shape, but you appear to have left the lees of the wine in it, for it's coated all over with some hard substance or other that I can't even scrape off with my nails. I'm not going to take it unless it's cleaned out first.'

So Peronella said:

'We made a bargain, and we'll stick to it. My husband will clean it out.'

'But of course,' said the husband. And having put down his tools and rolled up his sleeves, he called for a lamp and a scraping tool, lowered himself into the tub, and began to scrape away. Peronella, as though curious to see what he was doing, leaned over the mouth of the tub, which was not very wide, and resting her head on her arm and shoulder, she issued a stream of instructions, such as: 'Rub it up there, that's it, and there again!' and 'See if you can reach that teeny-weeny bit left at the top.'

While she was busy instructing and directing her husband in this fashion, Giannello, who had not fully gratified his desires that morning before the husband arrived, seeing that he couldn't do it in the way he wished, contrived to bring it off as best he could. So he went up to Peronella, who was completely blocking up the mouth of the tub, and in the manner of a wild and hot-blooded stallion mounting a Parthian mare in the open fields, he satisfied his young man's passion, which no sooner reached fulfilment than the scraping of the tub was completed, whereupon he stood back, Peronella withdrew her head from the tub, and the husband clambered out.

Then Peronella said to Giannello:

'Here, take this lamp, my good man, and see whether the job's been done to your satisfaction.'

Having taken a look inside the tub, Giannello told

her everything was fine, and he was satisfied. He then handed seven silver ducats to the husband, and got him to carry it round to his house.

Eighth Day

SIXTH STORY

Calandrino had a little farm not far from Florence, which he had received from his wife by way of a dowry. Among the other things he acquired from this farm, every year he used to obtain a pig there, and it was his regular custom to go to the country in December with his wife, slaughter the pig, and have it salted.

Now, it so happened that one year, when Calandrino's wife was not feeling very well, he went to the farm by himself to slaughter the pig. And when Bruno and Buffalmacco heard about this, knowing that his wife was remaining behind, they went to stay for a few days with a priest, who was a very great friend of theirs and lived near Calandrino's farm.

Calandrino had slaughtered the pig on the morning of the very day they arrived, and on seeing them with the priest, he called out to them, saying:

'I bid you a hearty welcome, my friends. Come along inside, and I'll show you what an excellent farmer I am.' And having taken them into the farmhouse, he showed them the pig.

It was a very fine pig, as they could see for themselves, and when they learnt from Calandrino that he intended to salt it and take it back to his family, Bruno said:

'You must be out of your mind! Why not sell it, so that we can all have a good time on the proceeds? You can always tell your wife it's been stolen.'

'Not a chance,' said Calandrino. 'She wouldn't believe me, and she'd kick me out of the house. Now, stop pestering me, because I shall never do anything of the sort.'

They argued with him at great length, but it was no use. And after Calandrino had invited them to stay for supper with so reluctant an air that they decided not to accept, they all took their leave of him.

After leaving Calandrino, Bruno said to Buffalmacco:

'Why don't we steal that pig of his tonight?'

'But how are we to do that?' said Buffalmacco.

'I've already thought of a good way to do it,' said Bruno, 'provided that he doesn't move it to some other place.'

'In that case,' said Buffalmacco, 'let's do it. After all, why not? And when the deed is done, you and I, and our friend the priest here, will all make merry together.'

The priest was very much in favour of this idea, and so Bruno said:

'This thing calls for a certain amount of finesse. Now you know, Buffalmacco, don't you, that Calandrino is a mean sort of fellow, who's very fond of drinking when other people pay. So let's go and take him to the tavern, where the priest can pretend to play the host to the rest of us and pay for all the drinks. When he sees that he has nothing to pay, Calandrino will drink himself into a stupor, and then the rest will be plain sailing because there's no one else staying at the house.'

Everything turned out as Bruno had predicted. When Calandrino saw that the priest would not allow him to pay, he began to drink like a fish, and quaffed a great deal more than he needed to make him drunk. By the time he left the tavern, it was already very late, and not wishing to eat any supper, he staggered off home and went to bed, thinking he had bolted the door whereas in fact he had left it wide open.

Buffalmacco and Bruno went and had supper with

the priest, and when the meal was over they stealthily made their way to Calandrino's house, taking with them certain implements so that they could break in at the spot that Bruno had decided on earlier in the day. On finding the door open, however, they walked in, collected the pig, and carted it off to the priest's house, where they stowed it away and went off to bed.

Next morning, having slept off the effects of the wine, Calandrino got up and went downstairs to find that his pig had gone and the door was open. So he went round asking various people whether they knew who had taken the pig, and being unable to find any trace of it, he began to make a great outcry, shouting: 'Alas! Woe is me! Somebody's stolen my pig!'

Meanwhile, Bruno and Buffalmacco got up and went round to Calandrino's to hear what he had to say about the pig. And no sooner did he catch sight of them than he called out to them, almost in tears, saying:

'Alas, my friends, somebody's stolen my pig.'

Bruno then went up to him, and, speaking out of the corner of his mouth, he said:

'Fancy that! So you've had a bit of sense at last, have you?'

'Pah!' exclaimed Calandrino. 'I'm telling you the gospel truth.'

'That's the way,' said Bruno. 'Go on shouting like that, so that people will think it's really happened.'

Whereupon Calandrino began to shout even louder, saying:

'God's body, man, I tell you it's been stolen, it really has.'

'Excellent, excellent,' said Bruno. 'Keep it up, give the thing plenty of voice and make yourself heard, so as to make it sound convincing.'

'You'll drive me to perdition in a minute,' said Calandrino. 'Do I have to hang myself by the neck before I can convince you that it really has been stolen?'

'Get away with you!' said Bruno. 'How can that be, when I saw it there myself only yesterday? Are you trying to make me believe it's flown away?'

'It's gone, I tell you,' said Calandrino.

'Go on,' said Bruno, 'you're joking.'

'I swear to you I'm telling the truth,' said Calandrino. 'What am I to do now? I can't go back home without the pig. My wife will never believe me, but even if she does, she'll make my life a misery for the next twelve months.'

'Upon my soul,' said Bruno, 'it's a serious business, if you're speaking the truth. But as you know, Calandrino, I was telling you only yesterday that you ought to say this. I wouldn't like to think that you were fooling your wife and us too at the same time.'

Calandrino protested loudly, saying:

'Ah! Why are you so intent on driving me to despair and provoking me to curse God and all the Saints in Heaven? I tell you the pig was stolen from me during the night.'

'If that's the case,' said Buffalmacco, 'we'll have to see if we can find some way of getting it back.'

'How are we to do that?' asked Calandrino.

So Buffalmacco said:

'Whoever took your pig, we can be quite sure that he didn't come all the way from India to do it. It must have been one of your neighbours. So all you have to do is to bring them all together so that I can give them the bread and cheese test, and we'll soon see who's got it.'

'Oh, yes,' said Bruno, 'your bread and cheese will work miracles, I'm sure, on some of the fine folk who live around here. It's quite obvious that one of them has the pig. They'd guess what we were up to, and stay away.'

'What's to be done, then?' asked Buffalmacco.

'What we ought to do,' Bruno replied, 'is to use the best ginger sweets we can get hold of, along with some fine Vernaccia wine, and invite them round for a drink. They wouldn't suspect anything, and they'd all turn up. And it's just as easy to bless ginger sweets as it is to bless bread and cheese.'

'You certainly have a point there,' said Buffalmacco. 'What do you say, Calandrino? Shall we give it a try?'

'Of course,' said Calandrino. 'Let's do that, for the love of God. If only I could find out who took it, I shouldn't feel half so miserable about it!'

'That's settled then,' said Bruno. 'Now I'd be quite willing to go to Florence and get these things for you, if you'll give me the money.'

Calandrino gave him all the money he had, which amounted to about forty pence, and so Bruno went to Florence and called on a friend of his, who was an apothecary. Having bought a pound of the best ginger sweets he had in stock, he got him to make two special ones, consisting of dog ginger seasoned with fresh hepatic aloes; then he had these coated with sugar, like the rest, and so as not to lose them or confuse them with the others, he had a tiny mark put on them which enabled him to recognize them without any difficulty. And having bought a flask of fine Vernaccia, he returned to Calandrino's place in the country, and said to him:

'See to it that you invite all the people you suspect to come and drink with you tomorrow morning. It's a holiday, so they'll all come readily enough. Tonight, along with Buffalmacco, I shall cast a spell on the sweets, and bring them round to your house first thing tomorrow morning. I shall hand the sweets out myself, to save you the trouble, and I shall pronounce all the right words and do all the right things.'

Calandrino issued the invitations, and next morning a goodly crowd of people assembled round the elm in front of the church, of whom some were farmworkers and others were young Florentines who happened to be staying in the country. Then along came Bruno and Buffalmacco with the box of sweets and the flask of wine, and having got them to stand in a circle, Bruno made the following announcement:

'Gentlemen, I must explain to you why you are here, so that if you should take offence at anything that happens, you won't go and blame it on me. The night before last, Calandrino, who is here among us, was robbed of a fine fat pig, and he can't find out who has taken it. And since it could only have been taken by one of the people here, he wants to discover who it was by offering, to each of you in turn, one of these sweets to eat, together with a drink of this wine. I should explain to you right away that whoever has taken the pig will be unable to swallow the sweet – in fact, he will find it more bitter than poison, and spit it out. So before he is put to so much shame in the presence of all these people, perhaps it would be better for the person responsible to make a clean breast of it to the priest, and I can call the whole thing off.'

All of them were only too eager to eat one of the sweets, and so Bruno, having lined them up with Calandrino in the middle, started from one end and began to hand one out to each of them in turn. When he came to Calandrino, he picked up one of the sweets of the canine variety and placed it in the palm of his hand. Calandrino promptly tossed it into his mouth and began to chew on it, but no sooner did his tongue come into contact with the aloe than, finding the bitter taste quite intolerable, he spat it out again.

They were all keeping a close watch on one another to see who was going to spit out his sweet, and Bruno, who still had several more to distribute, carried on as though nothing had happened until he heard a voice behind him saying: 'Hey, Calandrino, what's the meaning of this?' Turning quickly round, and seeing that Calandrino had spat his out, he said:

'Wait a minute! Perhaps he spat it out for some other reason. Here, take another!' And picking up the second one, he thrust it into Calandrino's mouth before proceeding to hand out the ones he had left.

Bitter as Calandrino had found the first, the second seemed a great deal more so, but being ashamed to spit it out, he kept it in his mouth for a while. As he chewed away at it, tears as big as hazelnuts began to roll down his cheeks until eventually, being unable to bear it any longer, he spat it out like the first.

Buffalmacco was meanwhile handing out drinks all round, with the assistance of Bruno. And when, along with all the others, they observed what had happened, everyone declared that Calandrino had obviously stolen the pig himself, and there were one or two who gave him a severe scolding about it.

However, when the crowd had dispersed, leaving

Bruno and Buffalmacco alone with Calandrino, Buffalmacco turned to him and said:

'I was convinced all along that you were the one who had taken it. You were just pretending to us that it had been stolen so that you wouldn't have to buy us a few drinks out of the proceeds.'

Calandrino, who still had the bitter taste of the aloe in his mouth, swore to them that he had not taken the pig, but Buffalmacco said:

'Own up, man, how much did it fetch? Six florins?'

Calandrino was by now on the brink of despair, but Bruno said:

'You might as well know, Calandrino, that one of the fellows we were drinking and eating with this morning told me that you had a girl up here, that you kept her for your pleasure and gave her all the little titbits that came your way, and that he was quite certain you had sent her this pig of yours. You've become quite an expert at fooling people, haven't you? Remember the time you took us along the Mugnone? There we were, collecting those black stones, and as soon as you'd got us stranded up the creek without a paddle, you cleared off home, and then tried to make us believe that you'd found the thing. And now that you've given away the pig, or sold it rather, you think you can persuade us, by uttering a few oaths, that it's been stolen. But you can't fool us any more: we've cottoned on to these tricks of yours. As a matter of fact, that's why we took so much trouble with the spell we cast on the sweets; and unless you give us two brace of capons for our pains, we intend to tell Monna Tessa the whole story.'

Seeing that they refused to believe him, and thinking that he had enough trouble on his hands without letting himself in for a diatribe from his wife, Calandrino gave them the two brace of capons. And after they had salted the pig, they carried their spoils back to Florence with them, leaving Calandrino to scratch his head and rue his losses.

Ninth Day

Some years ago, in Barletta, there was a priest called
Father Gianni di Barolo, who, because he had a poor
living and wished to supplement his income, took to
carrying goods, with his mare, round the various fairs
of Apulia, and to buying and selling. In the course of
his travels, he became very friendly with a man called
Pietro da Tresanti, who practised the same trade as his
own, but with a donkey, and in token of his friendship
and affection he always addressed him, in the Apulian
fashion, as Neighbour Pietro. And whenever Pietro
came to Barletta, Father Gianni always invited him to
his church, where he shared his quarters with him and
entertained him to the best of his ability.

For his own part, Neighbour Pietro was exceedingly
poor and had a tiny little house in Tresanti, hardly big
enough to accommodate himself, his donkey, and his
beautiful young wife. But whenever Father Gianni
turned up in Tresanti, he took him to his house and
entertained him there as best he could, in appreciation

of the latter's hospitality in Barletta. However, when it came to putting him up for the night, Pietro was unable to do as much for him as he would have liked, because he only had one little bed, in which he and his beautiful wife used to sleep. Father Gianni was therefore obliged to bed down on a heap of straw in the stable, alongside his mare and Pietro's donkey.

Pietro's wife, knowing of the hospitality which the priest accorded to her husband in Barletta, had offered on several occasions, when the priest came to stay with them, to go and sleep with a neighbour of hers called Zita Carapresa di Giudice Leo, so that the priest could sleep in the bed with her husband. But the priest wouldn't hear of it, and on one occasion he said to her:

'My dear Gemmata, don't trouble your head over me. I am quite all right, because whenever I choose I can transform this mare of mine into a fair young maid and turn in with her. Then when it suits me I turn her back into a mare. And that is why I'd never be without her.'

The young woman was astonished, believed every word of it, and told her husband, adding:

'If he's as good a friend as you say, why don't you

get him to teach you the spell, so that you can turn me into a mare and run your business with the mare as well as the donkey? We should earn twice as much money, and when we got home you could turn me back into a woman, as I am now.'

Being more of a simpleton than a sage, Neighbour Pietro believed all this and took her advice to heart; and he began pestering Father Gianni for all he was worth to teach him the secret. Father Gianni did all he could to talk him out of his folly, but without success, and so he said to him:

'Very well, since you insist, tomorrow we shall rise, as usual, before dawn, and I shall show you how it's done. To tell the truth, as you'll see for yourself, the most difficult part of the operation is to fasten on the tail.'

That night, Pietro and Gemmata were looking forward so eagerly to this business that they hardly slept a wink, and as soon as the dawn was approaching, they scrambled out of bed and called Father Gianni, who, having risen in his nightshirt, came to Pietro's tiny little bedroom and said:

'I know of no other person in the world, apart from yourself, for whom I would perform this favour, but as you continue to press me, I shall do it. However, if you want it to work, you must do exactly as I tell you.'

They assured him that they would do as he said. So Father Gianni picked up a lantern, handed it to Neighbour Pietro, and said:

'Watch me closely, and memorize carefully what I say. Unless you want to ruin everything, be sure not to utter a word, no matter what you may see or hear. And pray to God that the tail sticks firmly in place.'

Neighbour Pietro took the lantern and assured him he would do as he had said. Then Father Gianni got Gemmata to remove all her clothes and to stand on all fours like a mare, likewise instructing her not to utter a word whatever happened, after which he began to fondle her face and her head with his hands, saying:

'This be a fine mare's head.'

Then he stroked her hair, saying:

'This be a fine mare's mane.'

And stroking her arms, he said:

'These be fine mare's legs and fine mare's hooves.'

Then he stroked her breasts, which were so round and firm that a certain uninvited guest was roused and stood erect. And he said:

'This be a fine mare's breast.'

He then did the same to her back, her belly, her rump, her thighs and her legs: and finally, having nothing left to attend to except the tail, he lifted his shirt, took hold of the dibber that he did his planting with, and stuck it straight and true in the place made for it, saying:

'And this be a fine mare's tail.'

Until this happened, Neighbour Pietro had been closely observing it all in silence, but he took a poor view of this last bit of business, and exclaimed:

'Oh, Father Gianni, no tail! I don't want a tail!'

The vital sap which all plants need to make them grow had already arrived, when Father Gianni, standing back, said:

'Alas! Neighbour Pietro, what have you done? Didn't I tell you not to say a word no matter what you saw? The mare was just about to materialize, but now you've ruined everything by opening your mouth, and there's no way of ever making another.'

'That suits me,' said Neighbour Pietro. 'I didn't want the tail. Why didn't you ask me to do it? Besides, you stuck it on too low.'

To which Father Gianni replied:

'I didn't ask you because you wouldn't have known how to fasten it on, the first time, as deftly as I.'

The young woman, hearing these words, stood up and said to her husband, in all seriousness:

'Pah! what an idiot you are! Why did you have to ruin everything for the pair of us? Did you ever see a mare without a tail? So help me God, you're as poor as a church mouse already, but you deserve to be a lot poorer.'

Now that it was no longer possible to turn the young woman into a mare because of the words that Neighbour Pietro had uttered, she put on her clothes again, feeling all sad and forlorn. Meanwhile her husband prepared to return to his old trade, with no more than a donkey as usual: then he and Father Gianni went off to the fair at Bitonto together, and he never asked the same favour of him again.

Tenth Day

SECOND STORY

Ghino di Tacco, whose feats of daring and brigandage brought him great notoriety after being banished from Siena and incurring the enmity of the Counts of Santa Fiora, staged a rebellion in Radicofani against the Church of Rome; and having established himself in the town, he made sure that anyone passing through the surrounding territory was set upon and robbed by his marauders.

Now, the ruling Pope in Rome was Boniface VIII, and to his court there came the Abbot of Cluny, who was reputed to be one of the richest prelates in the world. In the course of his stay there, however, he ruined his stomach, and was advised by the physicians to go to the baths of Siena, where he was certain to recover. And so, having obtained permission from the Pope, he set out for Siena, heedless of the reputation of Ghino, accompanied by a huge and splendid train of goods, baggage, horses and servants.

On learning of his approach, Ghino di Tacco spread

out his nets, and without allowing so much as a single page-boy to escape, he cut off the Abbot with the whole of his retinue and belongings in a narrow gorge. This done, he dispatched his ablest lieutenant to the Abbot, suitably escorted, who very politely requested the Abbot, on his master's behalf, to be good enough to make his way to Ghino's fortress and dismount there. On hearing this, the Abbot flew into a terrible rage and replied that he had no intention of doing any such thing, as he had nothing to discuss with Ghino. In short, he was going to continue his journey, and would like to see anyone try to prevent him.

Whereupon Ghino's emissary, speaking in deferential tones, said to him:

'My lord, you have come to a place where except for the power of God we fear nothing, and where excommunications and interdicts are entirely ineffectual. Please be good enough, therefore, to comply with Ghino's wishes in this matter.'

Whilst these words were being exchanged, the whole place had been surrounded by brigands; and so the Abbot, realizing that he and his men were trapped, set off in high dudgeon with Ghino's emissary along the road leading to the fortress, together with all his goods and retinue. Having dismounted at a large house, he was lodged, on Ghino's instructions, in an extremely dark and uncomfortable little room, whereas all the others were given very comfortable quarters, each according to his rank, in various parts of the fortress. And as for the horses and all the Abbot's belongings, these were put in a safe place and left untouched.

Once this was done, Ghino went to the Abbot and said to him:

'My lord, I am sent by Ghino, of whom you are a guest, in order to ask whether you will be so good as to inform him where you were going, and for what reason.'

The Abbot, being a sensible man, had by this time swallowed his pride, and informed him where he was going and why, whereupon Ghino took his leave of him, and resolved to try and cure him without the aid of spa-waters. Having given instructions that the room should be closely guarded and that a large fire should be kept burning in the grate, he left the Abbot alone until the following morning, when he returned bringing him two slices of toasted bread wrapped in a spotless white cloth, together with a large glass of Corniglia wine from the Abbot's own stores. And he addressed the Abbot as follows:

'My lord, when Ghino was younger, he studied medicine, and he claims to have learnt that there is no better cure for the stomach-ache than the one he is about to administer, which begins with these things I have brought you. Take them, then, and be of good cheer.'

His hunger being greater than his appetite for jesting, the Abbot ate the bread and drank the wine, at the same time displaying his indignation. He then became very truculent, asked a number of questions, and issued a lot of advice; and he made a special point of asking to see Ghino.

Since much of what he had said was pointless, Ghino chose to ignore it; but to some of the Abbot's questions he gave polite answers, affirming that Ghino would visit him as soon as he could. Having given him this assurance, he took his leave, and a whole day elapsed before he returned, bringing the same quantity of toasted bread and Corniglia wine as before.

He kept him in this fashion for several days, until he perceived that the Abbot had eaten some dried beans, which he had deliberately left in the room after smuggling them in on an earlier visit.

He therefore asked the Abbot on Ghino's behalf whether his stomach seemed any better, to which the Abbot replied:

'It would seem to be all right, if only I were out of his clutches; and apart from that, my one great longing is to eat, so fully have his remedies restored me to health.'

Ghino therefore made arrangements for the Abbot's servants to furnish a stately chamber with the Abbot's own effects, and gave orders for a great banquet to be prepared, to which a number of the residents and all of the Abbot's retinue were invited. And next morning he went to the Abbot and said:

'My lord, since you are feeling well again, the time has come for you to leave the sick-room.' And taking him by the hand, he led him to the stately chamber and left him there with his own attendants, whilst he went off to make sure that the banquet would be truly magnificent.

The Abbot relaxed for a while in the company of his own folk, and described to them the sort of life he had been living, whereas they on the other hand declared of one accord that Ghino had entertained them lavishly. But the time having now arrived for them to eat, the Abbot and all the others were regaled with a succession of excellent dishes and superb wines, though Ghino still refrained from telling the Abbot who he was.

The Abbot was entertained in this way for several days running, but eventually Ghino gave instructions for all of his effects to be brought to a large room overlooking a courtyard where every one of the Abbot's horses was assembled, down to the most decrepit-looking nag he possessed. He then called on the Abbot and asked him how he was feeling and whether he was strong enough to travel. The Abbot replied that he was as strong as an ox, that he had fully recovered from his stomach ailment, and that once he was out of Ghino's hands, his troubles would be over.

Then Ghino took the Abbot to the room in which his goods and the whole of his retinue were gathered, and, guiding him to a window whence he could see all his horses, he said:

'My lord Abbot, you must realize that gentle birth, exile, poverty, and the desire to defend his life and his nobility against numerous powerful enemies, rather than any instinctive love of evil, have driven Ghino di Tacco, whom you see before you, to become a highway robber and an enemy of the court of Rome. But because you seem a worthy gentleman, and because I have cured you of the malady affecting your stomach, I do not intend to treat you as I would treat any other person who fell into my hands, of whose possessions I would take as large a portion as I pleased. On the contrary, I propose that you yourself, having given due regard to my needs, should decide how much or how little of your property you would care to leave with me. All your goods are set out here before you, and from this window you can see your horses tethered in the courtyard. I therefore bid you take as much or as little as you please, and you are henceforth free to leave whenever you wish.'

The Abbot was astonished and delighted to hear such generous sentiments from the lips of a highway robber, and promptly shed his anger and disdain, being filled instead with a feeling of goodwill towards Ghino, whom he was now disposed to look upon as a bosom friend. And he rushed to embrace him, saying:

'I swear to God that in order to win the friendship of such a man as I now judge you to be, I should willingly endure far greater wrongs than any you appear to have done me hitherto. A curse upon Fortune, that has compelled you to pursue so infamous a calling!'

Then the Abbot singled out an essential minimum of his numerous belongings and his horses, and leaving all the rest to Ghino, he returned to Rome.

The Pope had heard all about the seizure of the Abbot, and took a very serious view of the matter; but the first question he asked on seeing him again was whether the baths had done him any good. To which the Abbot replied, with a smile:

'Holy Father, without going as far as the baths I came across an excellent physician, who cured me completely.' He then described the manner of his cure, much to the pontiff's amusement; and he went on to ask the Pope, under the promptings of his generous instincts, to grant him a certain favour.

The Pope, thinking he would ask for something quite different, readily agreed to grant his request, whereupon the Abbot said:

'Holy Father, the favour I intend to ask of you is that you restore my physician, Ghino di Tacco, to your good graces, for he is assuredly one of the finest and worthiest men I have ever met. As to his wicked ways, I believe them to be more the fault of Fortune than his own; and if you will change his fortune by granting him the wherewithal to live in a style appropriate to his rank, I am convinced that within a short space of time, you will come to share my high opinion of him.'

The Pope was a person of lofty sentiments, always well disposed towards men of excellence, and he said that if Ghino was as fine a man as the Abbot claimed, he would gladly do as he was asked. And he told the Abbot to arrange for Ghino to come to Rome, it being perfectly safe for him to do so.

And so, in accordance with the Abbot's wishes, Ghino came to the papal court under safe conduct. Nor had he been there long before his worth was acknowledged by the Pope, who made peace with him and granted him a large priory in the Order of the Hospitallers, having first created him a Knight of that Order. This position he held for the rest of his days, remaining a friend and servant of Mother Church and the Abbot of Cluny.

PENGUIN 60s CLASSICS

PENGUIN 60s CLASSICS

HENRY JAMES · *The Lesson of the Master*
FRANZ KAFKA · *The Judgement*
THOMAS À KEMPIS · *Counsels on the Spiritual Life*
HEINRICH VON KLEIST · *The Marquise of O—*
LIVY · *Hannibal's Crossing of the Alps*
NICCOLÒ MACHIAVELLI · *The Art of War*
SIR THOMAS MALORY · *The Death of King Arthur*
GUY DE MAUPASSANT · *Boule de Suif*
FRIEDRICH NIETZSCHE · *Zarathustra's Discourses*
OVID · *Orpheus in the Underworld*
PLATO · *Phaedrus*
EDGAR ALLAN POE · *The Murders in the Rue Morgue*
ARTHUR RIMBAUD · *A Season in Hell*
JEAN-JACQUES ROUSSEAU · *Meditations of a Solitary Walker*
ROBERT LOUIS STEVENSON · *Dr Jekyll and Mr Hyde*
TACITUS · *Nero and the Burning of Rome*
HENRY DAVID THOREAU · *Civil Disobedience*
LEO TOLSTOY · *The Death of Ivan Ilyich*
IVAN TURGENEV · *Three Sketches from a Hunter's Album*
MARK TWAIN · *The Man That Corrupted Hadleyburg*
GIORGIO VASARI · *Lives of Three Renaissance Artists*
EDITH WHARTON · *Souls Belated*
WALT WHITMAN · *Song of Myself*
OSCAR WILDE · *The Portrait of Mr W. H.*

ANONYMOUS WORKS

Beowulf and Grendel
Gilgamesh and Enkidu
Tales of Cú Chulaind

Buddha's Teachings
Krishna's Dialogue on the Soul
Two Viking Romances